We Love Holidays
ID-UL-FITR

Saviour Pirotta

PowerKiDS
press.
New York

Saviour Pirotta is a highly experienced author, who has written many books for young children. He was born in Malta and is also a trained chef.

Published in 2008 by The Rosen Publishing Group, Inc.
29 East 21st Street, New York, NY 10010

First Edition

The publishers would like to thank the following for allowing us to reproduce their pictures in this book:

Wayland Picture Library: 12 / Alamy: 4, 19, ArkReligion.com; 5, Tina Manley; title page, 9, 11, Sally and Richard Greenhill; 13, 17, World Religions Photo Library / Corbis: 6, Thomas Hartwell; 10, Mian Khursheed; 14, Reuters / World Religions Photo Library: 7, 8, 18, 20, 21, 22, Christine Osborne; 15, 23, cover, Paul Gapper; 16. Richard Bell;

Library of Congress Cataloging-in-Publication Data

Pirotta, Saviour.
    Id-ul-Fitr / Saviour Pirotta. -- 1st ed.
      p. cm. -- (We love holidays)
    Includes index.
    ISBN-13: 978-1-4042-3708-7 (library binding)
    ISBN-10: 1-4042-3708-9 (library binding)
    1. 'Id al-Fitr--Juvenile literature. 2. Ramadan--Juvenile literature. 3. Fasts and feasts--Islam--Juvenile literature. I. Title.
    BP186.45.P57 2007
    297.3'6--dc22
                                    2006026801

Manufactured in China

Contents

Welcome to Id

Salaam Alaikum—peace be upon you. Welcome to the holy month of Ramadan, and to Id-ul-Fitr, the biggest festival in the Islamic year.

People ▶ send greeting cards to their friends and family at Id.

4

Ramadan is the month when the angel Jibril gave the prophet Muhammad ﷺ the words of Allah, the One God. These were written in the Koran. Muslims celebrate Ramadan to remember this very special month.

This girl has decorated her hands with henna patterns for the Id celebrations.

5

Fasting in Ramadan

During Ramadan, Muslims try to grow closer to Allah by reading the Koran and praying. They are careful not to say anything bad about anyone, or to listen to gossip about other people.

Muslim children go to school as usual at Ramadan.
▶

6

Grown up Muslims and older children also fast between sunrise and sunset. That means they have no food or drink, not even water.

Extra prayers are said throughout the day, in the month of Ramadan.
◄

Beginning the fast

Everyone wakes up before dawn, and families eat a meal called Suhur. The food varies from country to country.

At dawn, people are called to prayer at the mosque and the fasting begins. ▶

In Egypt, many people have a simple
breakfast of bread, yogurt, cheese,
and tea. Suhur must be finished before
sunrise.

Breaking the fast

When the sun goes down, Muslims break their fast and eat. Many choose a handful of dates and some water. That's how the Prophet Muhammad ﷺ broke his fast.

Later in the evening, they have a bigger
meal called Ifthar. They may invite
friends to share it. Ifthar meals are
delicious. In many countries, people
cook special Ramadan dishes.

The holiest night

Toward the end of Ramadan comes a very special night called the Night of Power, or Laylat-ul-Qadr. Muslims consider it the holiest night of the year. They believe it's when the angel Jibril started revealing the Koran to the Prophet ﷺ.

Some Muslims spend the last ten days of Ramadan at the mosque.
▶

Muslims believe that all wrongdoings are forgiven on the Night of Power.

Many Muslims spend all night praying and reading the Koran at the mosque.

◄ The Koran is believed to show God's own words. This one has been carefully decorated.

A new moon, a new celebration

When the moon appears in this crescent shape, it is known as a new moon.
▶

Fasting ends on the last day of Ramadan. The first day of the next month, Shawwal sees the celebration of Id-ul-Fitr. It starts when the new moon appears in the sky.

People wear brand new clothes for Id. They go to the mosque where everybody greets each other with the words "Id Mubarak," "Blessed Id," "Happy Id."

Muslims make sure they look their best for Id. ◀

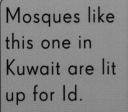

At the mosque

At the mosque there is a special Id prayer. Everyone says it together. Then the Imam prays for all Muslims around the world. Everyone hugs friends and relatives.

Mosques like this one in Kuwait are lit up for Id.
▼

d is a time for thinking of others. Before the Id prayer starts, everyone gives some money for the poor.

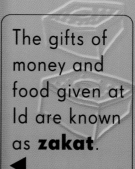

The gifts of money and food given at Id are known as **zakat**.
◀

DID YOU KNOW?

The special "night prayer" that is recited at the mosque is called the Taraweeh.

Id mubarak

Id is mostly a family celebration. Many people decorate their homes with stars and moons. Some fill it with flowers.

In many countries, there are street festivals with music and dancing. ▶

This family has dressed in their best clothes for an Id festival in Malaysia.

Everyone sends Id cards and visits friends and relatives. Those who have argued during the year make up and shake hands.

DID YOU KNOW?

Children receive presents, new clothes, and sometimes gifts of money, too.

Treats at Id

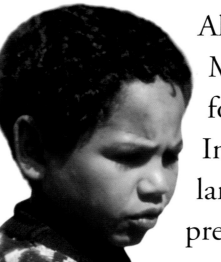

All over the world, Muslims have special food to celebrate Id. In Iraq, they have roast lamb, but in Egypt they prefer fish.

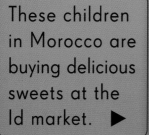

These children in Morocco are buying delicious sweets at the Id market. ▶

After fasting at Ramadan, Muslims
look forward to special treats at Id.
Iraqis and Palestinians make special
pastry cases filled with chopped dates.
In Indonesia, they have a rich cake
with vanilla and spices.

▲
These special
starters have
been laid
out for a
wonderful
Id feast.

End of Id

The Id feast is the first time in a month that many have eaten during the day. Afterward, they thank Allah for helping them keep the fast through Ramadan.

These Muslims in Tanzania are celebrating Id with music and singing.
▼

It has made them think about people less lucky than themselves. It has also made them feel close to all other Muslims around the world.

Friends and relatives hug and greet each other at Id.

Index

Glossary

Allah the Muslim name for God
fast to go without food or drink
henna a red dye used to decorate skin and color hair
Ifthar the evening meal that Muslims have during Ramadan
Iman a Muslim religious leader
Koran the Holy Book of Islam
Mosque the building where Muslims meet for worship
Prophet someone who gives people messages from God
Ramadan the month in the Islamic year when people fast
Suhur the meal eaten before sunrise during Ramadan
Zakat special gifts of money or food that are given to the poor

Due to the changing nature of Internet links, Powerkids Press has developed an online list of Web sites related to the subject of this book. This site is updated regularly. Please use this link to access the list: www.powerkidslinks.com/wlf/id/